BIG CHICKENS
FLY THE COOP

LESLIE HELAKOSKI ✳ illustrated by HENRY COLE

SCHOLASTIC INC.
New York Toronto London Auckland Sydney
Mexico City New Delhi Hong Kong Buenos Aires

ISBN-13: 978-0-545-15128-3
ISBN-10: 0-545-15128-7

Text copyright © 2008 by Leslie Helakoski.
Illustrations copyright © 2008 by Henry Cole.
All rights reserved. Published by Scholastic Inc., 557 Broadway, New York, NY 10012, by arrangement with Dutton Children's Books, a division of Penguin Young Readers Group, a member of Penguin Group (USA) Inc. SCHOLASTIC and associated logos are trademarks and/or registered trademarks of Scholastic Inc.

12 11 10 9 8 7 6 5 4 3 2 1   9 10 11 12 13 14/0

Printed in the U.S.A.   40

First Scholastic printing, March 2009

Designed by Heather Wood

To my daughter Claire
and all her journeys

— L. H.

For Teensy:
My coop runneth over!

— H. C.

FOUR BIG chickens sat on their nests and sighed.

"It's nice and safe at home in the coop," said one chicken.

"Yes," said the others.

"We should always stay home."

"We could always stay home."

"We would always stay home . . . except . . . we've always wanted to see the farmhouse."

"That's true," said the chickens, and they climbed out of their nests and headed out of the coop.

Partway across the farmyard,
the chickens stopped.

"Is that the farmhouse?" asked
one chicken.

"It has a roof."

They tiptoed closer.

"It has a door."

They stuck their necks out.

"It has a *tail*?"

"It's a doghouse!"

The chickens flounced,
trounced, and body-bounced.
The dogs pounced. Drooling
muzzles dribbled. Frightened
yard birds quibbled. Sharp teeth
crashed. Pointed beaks smashed.
Snouts snapped. Wings flapped.
Until . . .

. . . four slobbery chickens ran all the way back to the coop.

"We should've stayed home."

"We could've stayed home."

"We would've stayed home . . .

except . . .

. . . we want to taste the bugs at the farmhouse."

"That's true," said the chickens, and they headed out of the coop.

Partway across the farmyard, the chickens stopped.

"Is that the farmhouse?" asked one chicken.

"It has a chimney."

They tiptoed closer.

"It has a seat."

They stuck their necks out.

"It has four *tires*?"

"It's a tractor!"

The chickens scritched, hitched, and flip-switched. The tractor twitched into life. The rusty engine roared. Startled heartbeats soared. Black smoke spewed. Foul moods brewed. Eyes burned. Guts churned. Until . . .

. . . four sooty chickens ran all the
way back to the coop.

   "We should've stayed home."

   "We could've stayed home."

   "We would've stayed home . . .

except . . .

. . . we want to see the view from the farmhouse."

"That's true," said the chickens, and they headed out of the coop.

Partway across the farmyard, they stopped.

"Is that the farmhouse?" asked one chicken.

"It has a gate."

They tiptoed closer.

"It has a window."

They stuck their necks out.

"It has *hay*?"

"It's a barn!"

The chickens stomped, whomped, and clompity-clomped. The horses chomped at the bit. Skittish ponies bolted. Frazzled feathers molted. Hard shoes kicked. Wing tips flicked. Manes whipped. Tails flipped. Until . . .

. . . four saddle-sore chickens ran all the way back to the coop.

The chickens sat on their nests and sighed.

"We'll never get to the farm-house," said one chicken.

"No," said the others.

"The dogs are too loud."

"The tractor's too dirty."

"The horses are too wild."

The chickens sighed again.

"It's too hard . . . except . . .

. . . chickens can be loud."

"Chickens can be dirty."

"Chickens can be wild."

"That's true," said the chickens. "And we really want to see the farmhouse."

Four big chickens climbed out of their nests and headed out of the coop.

When the dogs barked, the
chickens fluttered over the fence
and landed . . .

. . . on the tractor.
When the tractor smoked, the
chickens flopped off and landed . . .

. . . on the horse's back.
When the horse bucked, the
chickens flipped off and landed . . .

. . . in front of a house.

"Is that the farmhouse?" asked
one chicken.

"It has a roof; it has a door; it
has a chimney; it has a seat; it
has a window; it has a gate. It
MUST be the farmhouse!"

The chickens bugged, slugged,
and bear-hugged. They viewed,
shooed, and woo-hooed. They
stayed, played, and egg-laid. All
day long, the chickens glanced,
pranced, and tap-danced until . . .

. . . they noticed their own coop
right next door.

"Did someone move our coop?"

"It must be true," said the chickens.
"And now we can go to the farmhouse anytime we want."

Four slobbery, sooty, saddle-sore chickens
strutted all the way home.